Pi-shu

the little panda

For Holly

Published by
PEACHTREE PUBLISHERS, LTD.
1700 Chattahoochee Avenue
Atlanta, Georgia 30318-2112

www.peachtree-online.com

Text and illustrations © 2001 by John Butler

First published in Great Britain in 2001 by Orchard Books.

Printed and bound in China

10 9 8 7 6 5 4 3 2 1
First Edition

ISBN 1-56145-242-4

Cataloging-in-Publication Data is available from the Library of Congress

Pi-shu

the little panda

John Butler

On the slopes of Misty Mountain, in central China, a mother panda cuddled her tiny baby. Hidden in the hollow trunk of an old tree, she washed him and fed him with her warm milk as he snuggled happily into her thick, soft fur. His name was Pi-shu, and he was no bigger than one of the patches around his mother's eyes.

Pi-shu was born with a little pink tail, which would slowly disappear as he grew. His mother Fei-Fei thought he was the most beautiful panda she had ever seen.

Fei-Fei never left Pi-shu
alone for long, and she
would often cradle him
gently in her strong arms.

As Pi-shu grew into a little furry bundle, Fei-Fei carried him around on her back. At six months he had learned to walk on his own, and he started to copy his mother, chewing on bamboo shoots. Pi-shu liked the taste and the rough feel of the bamboo in his mouth. In another three months he no longer needed his mother's milk.

By his first birthday Pi-shu
was strong and adventurous.
Everywhere he looked there
were things to play with...

trees to climb...

frogs that jumped
when he sniffed them...

bamboo rats that played hide-and-seek in and out of their burrows.

One day, as early winter storms gathered over
the mountains, Pi-shu saw a troop of golden
monkeys high in the treetops. He followed them
as they leapt gracefully from tree to tree.

Pi-shu trotted after the monkeys as fast as he could. The little panda had never been so far down the mountainside before. As he pushed through some thick ferns, a smoky smell warned him to stop. He could hear a harsh chopping noise and strange, loud voices.

Pi-shu froze as a huge crash shook the ground under his feet. A tree had fallen. Peering out from the ferns, he saw that he was at the very edge of the forest. Men had stripped away almost all of the trees to grow crops of rice and corn, and they were chopping down more trees to burn on their winter fires. Frightened, Pi-shu turned and ran back to find his mother.

Pi-shu scrambled through the undergrowth. He came to a small clearing in the forest, and nearly ran into a takin, grazing with her baby. They stared at each other in surprise before Pi-shu scampered on, still looking for his mother.

When Pi-shu found Fei-Fei, he rushed to her side.
She could see that he was very afraid. She sensed
that this part of the forest wasn't safe anymore. It
was time to leave.

Early the next morning Pi-shu and Fei-Fei set off, climbing higher and higher until they reached a misty plateau. Their oily fur kept them warm, but it was hard work clambering over the slippery rocks, especially for little Pi-shu.

With the first snows beginning to fall, Pi-shu and Fei-Fei crossed the high alpine meadow and headed toward the next valley. It looked quiet and peaceful far below. Resting against the cold, hard rocks, they slept as best they could.

They awoke the next day to a blanket
of snow. Slowly the pandas descended the
steep slope into the valley, feeding on
bamboo as they came to it.

It was evening when Pi-shu and Fei-Fei reached the valley floor and found a clear mountain stream near a lush grove of bamboo. They ate their fill and settled into a contented sleep as darkness fell.

One day Pi-shu would want to climb other mountains and find a place of his own to live, but right now he didn't want to change a thing, not for all the bamboo in China.

Panda Facts

Pi-shu is an ancient Chinese name for panda, meaning "brave." Giant pandas are found only in the dense bamboo forests of the mountainous regions in China. Panda babies are usually born as twins and are about four inches long at birth. Often only the stronger of the two cubs survives.

A giant panda eats around thirty pounds of bamboo a day to keep alive, though some have been recorded eating as much as eighty-four pounds in a day—nearly half their bodyweight. Pandas eat different types of bamboo at different times of the year, mainly arrow bamboo in winter and umbrella bamboo in summer.

Giant pandas are among the rarest animals in the world. There are only about one thousand of them left in the wild. Their numbers have decreased mainly because of the growth in human population and the destruction of the panda's natural habitat.

The giant panda is an endangered species. To learn more about the conservation and protection of giant pandas, contact:

World Wildlife Fund, *www.worldwildlife.org*
1-800-CALL-WWF, 1250 24th Street NW, Washington, DC 20077-7795